# I'm a Good Citizen

Jayden Coll-Seck

Rosen REAL READERS

Rosen Classroom™
New York

My name is Kim.

I live in the United States.

I am a United States citizen.

This is my mom and dad.
They teach me how to
be a good citizen.

Mom and dad teach me
that it is important to follow laws.
I follow the laws
in my community.

I do not litter.
Littering is against the law.
I throw my trash
in the garbage can.

I pick up litter with my mom.
We like to keep
our neighborhood clean.

My parents say that being a good citizen means helping others.

I like to help others.

I bring groceries to my neighbor.

My family likes to
help others too.
We have a bake sale
to raise money.

People come to the bake sale.
They buy our baked goods.

We made over 50 dollars
at our bake sale!
We will donate the money
to a charity.

It feels good to help people.

It feels good to be a good citizen!

# Words to Know

dad

family

litter

mom

money

neighbor